Dot and Mit

by Bobby Lynn Maslen
pictures by John R. Maslen

Scholastic Inc.
New York • Toronto • London • Auckland • Sydney • Mexico City • New Delhi • Hong Kong • Buenos Aires

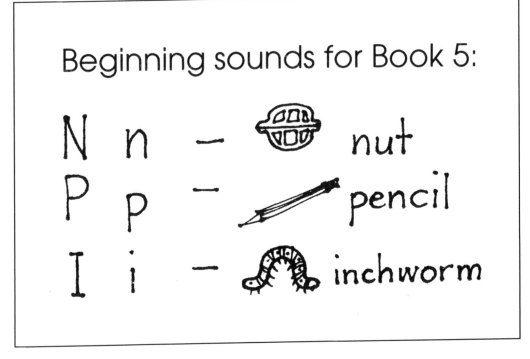

Beginning sounds for Book 5:

N n — nut

P p — pencil

I i — inchworm

Ask for Bob Books at your local bookstore, or visit www.bobbooks.com.

Thank you to Larry Sims, trumpeter for all ages, and to our editor and navigator, Shannon Penney.

ISBN-10: 0-545-01919-2
ISBN-13: 978-0-545-01919-4

Dot and Mit: ISBN 0-545-02718-7
Dot and the Dog: ISBN 0-545-02719-5
Jig and Mag: ISBN 0-545-02720-9
Muff and Ruff: ISBN 0-545-02721-7

6 5 4 3 2 1   7 8 9 10 11/0

Printed in China
This edition first printing, October 2007

Dot has a cat.

The cat is Mit.

Dot and Mit sit on a mat.

Dot is hot. Mit is hot.

Dot did nap.

Mit did not nap.

"Sit, Dot."

Dot did not nap.

The End

Dot and the Dog

by Bobby Lynn Maslen
pictures by John R. Maslen

Scholastic Inc.
New York • Toronto • London • Auckland • Sydney • Mexico City • New Delhi • Hong Kong • Buenos Aires

Book 6 adds:

question mark

?

14

Dot had a bag.

The bag had a tag.

Is the bag hot?
The bag is hot.

Dot had a dog. The dog is Mag.
Mag got the bag. Dot got Mag.

18

Dot sat. Did Mag sit?
Mag sat on the bag.

Mag hid the bag.

Dot got Mag and the bag.

The bag had a hot dog.

The End

Jig and Mag

by Bobby Lynn Maslen
pictures by John R. Maslen

Scholastic Inc.
New York • Toronto • London • Auckland • Sydney • Mexico City • New Delhi • Hong Kong • Buenos Aires

Beginning sounds for Book 7:

J j –  jar

W w – watch

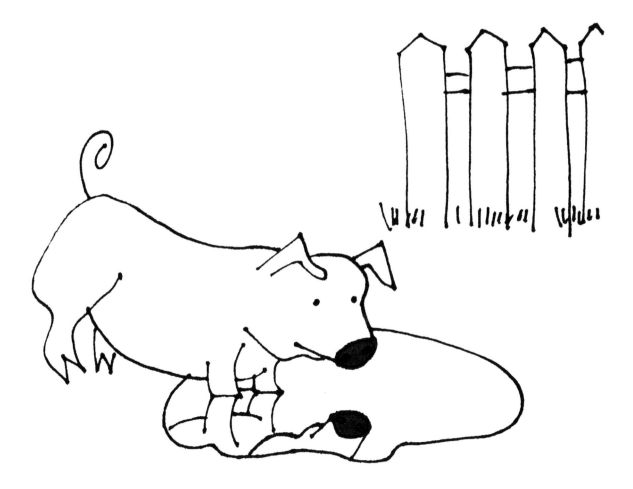

Jig is a big pig.

Jig can dig and dig.

Mag can dig and dig.

Did Jig win? Did Mag win?

Jig did win.

Jig and Mag ran.

Mag can tag Jig.

Mag did win.

The End

Muff and Ruff

by Bobby Lynn Maslen
pictures by John R. Maslen

Scholastic Inc.
New York • Toronto • London • Auckland • Sydney • Mexico City • New Delhi • Hong Kong • Buenos Aires

Beginning sounds for Book 8:

U u – umbrella

F f – feather

Muff and Ruff tug a rag rug.

Mac ran to Ruff.

Mac, Muff, and Ruff tug.

Rip it up, Ruff.

Nip at it, Muff.

Ruff hid in it.

Muff and Mac sat on it.

A rag rug is fun for
Muff, Ruff, and Mac.